This book belongs to

Dino Dance

Shimmer and Shine

nickelodeon

One day, Leah and Zac were busy searching every inch of Leah's backyard.

"I can't find my Artie Apatosaurus anywhere," Zac said. He really liked his dinosaur toy and wanted to get it back.

They checked behind the trashcan, in the trashcan, in the birdbath—everywhere!

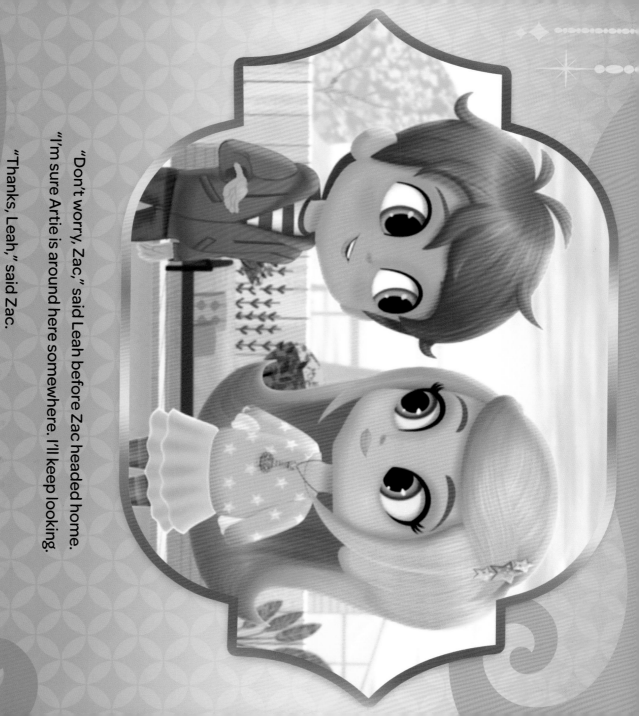

"Don't worry, Zac," said Leah before Zac headed home.
"I'm sure Artie is around here somewhere. I'll keep looking."

"Thanks, Leah," said Zac.

Leah checked under Zac's dog, Rocket. No toy dino.

Then she got a good idea! She had a special necklace with an amazing power.

"I can ask my genies for help!" she said. But she couldn't let Zac know she had genies! It was their secret.

In Zahramay Falls, where Shimmer and Shine lived, the bracelets of the twin genies-in-training started to glow!

"You know what that means?" asked Shimmer.

"It's time to see our friend Leah!" cheered Shine.

Shimmer and Shine,
My genies divine,
Through this special chant,
Three wishes you'll grant.

I'm Shimmer.
I'm Shine.
Your genies divine!
Boom Zahramay!
Your best friends
are on the way.

Up and away went Shimmer and Shine on their magic carpet with Tala the monkey and Nahal the tiger cub.

Poof!

The genies poofed right out of Leah's necklace bottle.

"I'm so glad you guys are here," said Leah. "My friend Zac lost his Artie Apatosaurus and we can't find it."

"Patty-o . . . a-pat-o-what's-it?" asked Shine.

Leah giggled. "Ar-tie A-pat-o-saur-us," she pronounced. "That's Zac's favorite dinosaur toy, and it's missing. I've checked everywhere for it."

Boom Zahramay! First wish of the day! Shimmer and Shine—Artie Apatosaurus divine!

"Ooh! I have an idea!" offered Shimmer. "You can use one of your three wishes to get Zac a new dinosaur, Leah."

"That's a great idea, Shimmer," agreed Leah. "For my first wish, I wish for an Artie Apatosaurus!"

Leah gasped! Standing in her yard was a living, breathing dinosaur!

"It's so big!" she exclaimed.

The dinosaur stomped and screeched.

"And loud!" said Shimmer.

"And *adorable!*" squealed Shine.

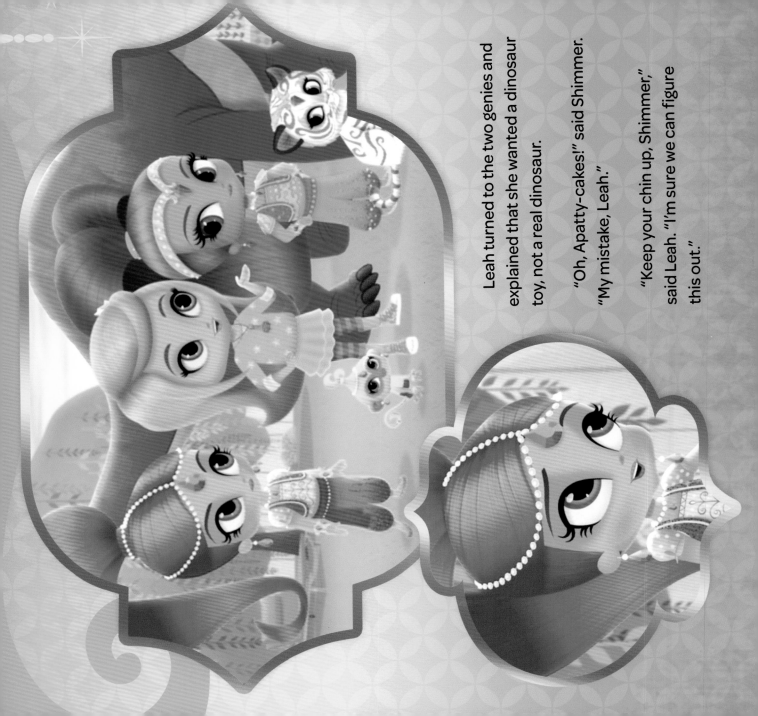

Leah turned to the two genies and explained that she wanted a dinosaur toy, not a real dinosaur.

"Oh, Apatty-cakes!" said Shimmer. "My mistake, Leah."

"Keep your chin up, Shimmer," said Leah. "I'm sure we can figure this out."

"You can make another wish, Leah," suggested Shimmer.

"Just say the magic words," added Shine.

"Okay," said Leah. "For my second wish, I wish for a dinosaur toy."

Boom Zahramay!
Second wish of the day!
Shimmer and Shine—
dinosaur toy divine!

Poof!

Shine clapped her hands and a big ball of yarn appeared.

"Since a ball of yarn is Nahal's favorite toy," said Shine, "I thought Artie might want one, too."

"I'm glad Artie likes his toy," said Leah, "but what I was hoping for was a toy dinosaur for Zac. Not a toy for a dinosaur."

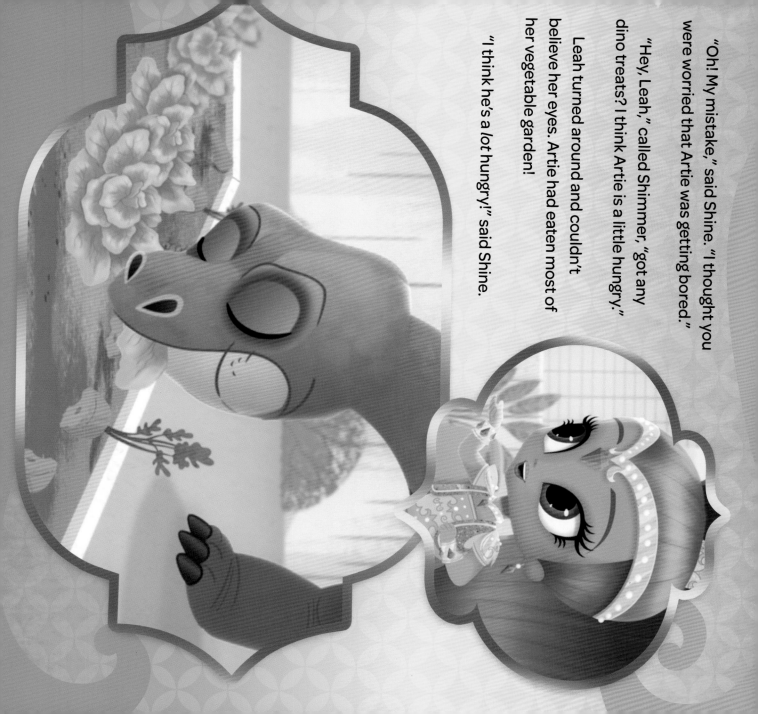

"Oh! My mistake," said Shine. "I thought you were worried that Artie was getting bored."

"Hey, Leah," called Shimmer, "got any dino treats? I think Artie is a little hungry."

Leah turned around and couldn't believe her eyes. Artie had eaten most of her vegetable garden!

"I think he's a *lot* hungry!" said Shine.

Then Artie began to munch on the apple tree that grew in Zac's backyard!

"You know what they say," said Shine: "An apple a day makes a dino okay."

"I've never heard you say that before," said Shimmer.

"That's 'cause I just made it up!" replied Shine.

Meanwhile, Zac was having a snack in his backyard when suddenly he looked up.

"Huh," he said to himself. "For a second there, I thought I saw a dinosaur chowing down on my apple tree . . ."

Poof!

The genies had coaxed Artie away from Zac's tree—*Poof!*—with a magical tree with apple pie, apple juice, and caramel apples!

Artie loved that tree! And the genies loved playing with Artie.

"It's probably time for Artie to head home," said Leah. "For my third wish, I wish this dinosaur was—

But Artie kept roaring—*ROAR!*

"I said, I wish he was—"

ROAR!

"I said, I wish—Oh, I wish Artie would stop roaring," Leah said with a sigh.

"Boom Zahramay! Third wish of the day!" cheered Shimmer.

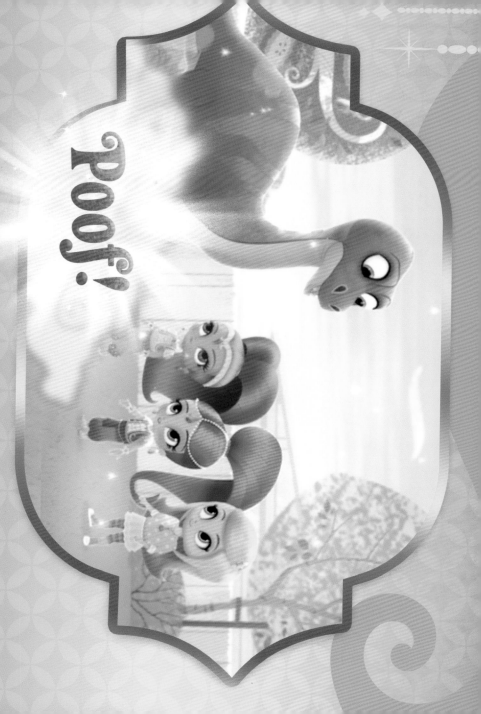

Poof!

"Wait!" exclaimed Leah, realizing what she had just done. "That's my last wish!"

"Shimmer and Shine—stop roaring divine!" commanded Shimmer.

Poof!

Artie started to roar and . . . "Meow" . . . came out.

"See?" said Shimmer. "No more roaring. Isn't that adorable?"

"Aww. He sounds just like Nahal," gushed Shine.

"*Meow...*" repeated Artie.

"He is cute," agreed Leah, "but we're still missing a toy for Zac, and there's a giant dinosaur in my backyard." She watched in dismay as Artie romped around the yard.

"I know," said Shimmer. "We could train him!" Then, with a snap of her fingers she conjured a book called *Training a Dinosaur: Genie Style.*

The genies were great animal trainers. They taught Artie how to roll over, shake hands, and even dance!

"This dino's got moves like you've never seen before," said Shimmer.

Poof! Artie was in the groove!

"That's it, Artie!" called Shine. "Do the robot!"

Suddenly, Zac came into the yard. Oh, no! The genies quickly hid behind a tree.

"Whoa!" exclaimed Zac. "Was that dinosaur just dancing like a robot? That is so awesome! I can't believe you have a robot dinosaur! It looks so real. How did you get one of these, Leah?"

"I was looking for your Artie Apatosaurus," Leah explained, "but this is the closest I could get to a dinosaur toy."

Zac nodded. "It happens. Happens a lot."

"Can we turn it back on?" asked Zac. "I wanna dance with the robo-dino."

And so Zac grooved with the "robo-dino," never realizing that two genies were showing Artie what moves to make. They stomped and stepped until —oops!—Artie lost his balance, fell into a bush, and the dance ended.

Crash!

"That was a blast!" said Zac. "I wish my Artie Apatosaurus toy was here to see it."

"Zac!" said Leah, pointing to the ground under the bush. "He *is* here!"

"Artie Apatosaurus!" exclaimed Zac, scooping the toy off the ground. "I missed him so much! Thanks for helping me find him, Leah."

As Zac left for home, Leah turned to her genie friends. "Thanks for all your help. If we hadn't made the mistake of wishing up a real dinosaur, we wouldn't have found the toy dinosaur."

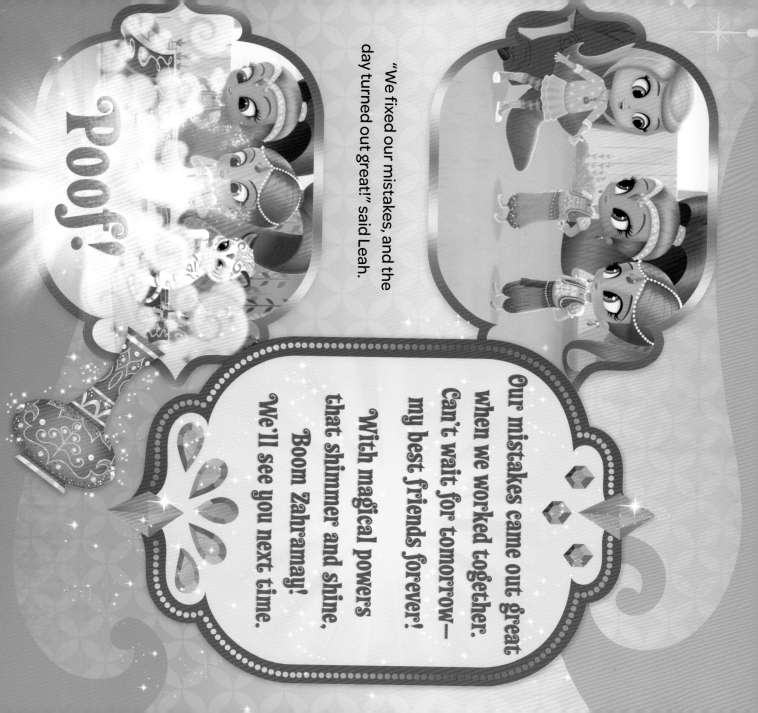

Poof!

"We fixed our mistakes, and the day turned out great!" said Leah.

Our mistakes came out great when we worked together. Can't wait for tomorrow— my best friends forever!

With magical powers that shimmer and shine, Boom Zahramay! We'll see you next time.

Back in Zahramay Falls, the genies were practicing tricks with Tala, Nahal, and their new pet, Artie, when . . .

Oof!—they all landed on the pillows.

"We need to work on that!" giggled Shimmer and Shine.